# Knock! Knock!

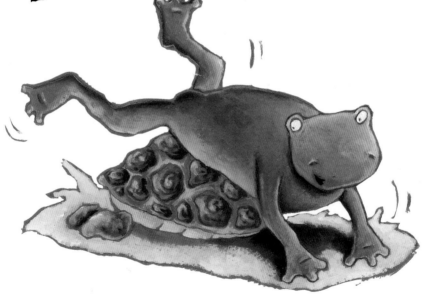

**written by Judith Nicholls**
**illustrated by Stefania Colnaghi**

**Ladybird**

said the chick.
"Is it a rock?
Is it a brick?

Come here, Duck," said the chick. "Come and look!

"It's a          said the duck.

"Come here, Dog!" said the duck.

"Come here,

said the chick.

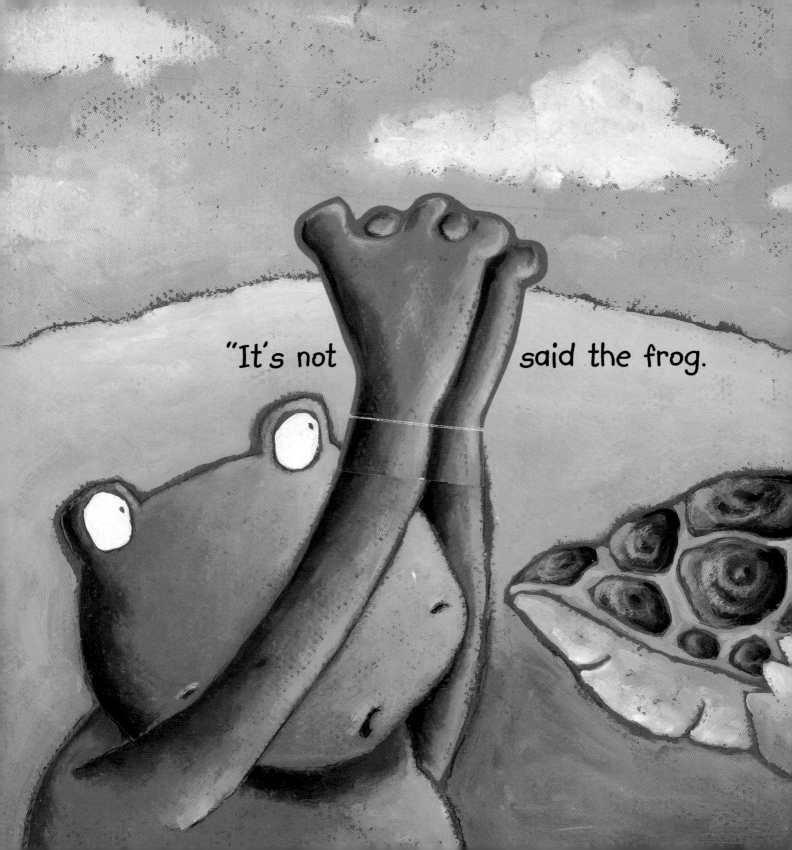

"It's quite small," said the frog.

"Did it drop from the

"Don't fall!" said the chick.
"It must be a brick."

"Stand back!"
said the

"It's a trick!" said the

"Get my stick!" said the dog.

"Will it    said the frog.

said the chick.

ck!
ick!"

said the duck.

said the dog.

"Look out!" said the frog.

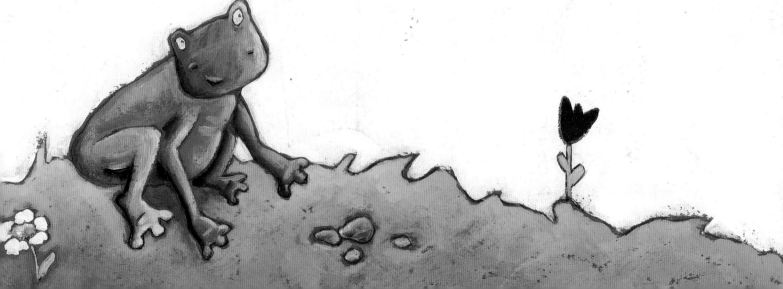

"It IS just a rock," said the frog and the

But the rock said...

Put a feather on the edge of a table. With your mouth close to the feather, say some of the flap words from the story: (Knock, duck, chick, quack). Does the feather move when you say the words? Which word makes the feather move the most?

Play the 'knock! Knock! I'm a rock' game. The first player says, "Knock! Knock!" and then a word that rhymes with rock: "Knock! knock! I'm a clock!" The second player says, "knock! knock! I'm a..." and chooses a different rhyming word to finish the sentence.

Say, "Knock! Knock!" like the chick. Now say it like the duck, the dog and the frog. Whose voice is the lowest? Whose voice is the highest?

Lots of the words in this story end with the letters 'ck'. See how many times you can find these two letters together.